This Makes Me Silly

SCHOLASTIC INC.

Today I am going
to the zoo
with my family.

I cannot wait
to see the animals!

A tour guide
shows us around.
She pretends to talk
to some ducklings.

It makes me laugh.
My heart feels
warm and fuzzy
like their feathers.

We see elephants
playing in the water.
They have long trunks.

My brother and I act
like elephants, too.
My insides feel wiggly
like their trunks!

Next we see lions.
Our guide asks
if we know how to roar.

The answer is yes!
We all roar
as loud as we can.

Then we see the monkeys.
They make funny faces.
We make funny faces, too.

The monkeys get angry!
The tour guide tells us
not to tease them.

Soon it is time
for lunch.

We have
a family picnic!
I feel as light
as a bird.

My brother eats
his banana
like a monkey.

I laugh so hard that water goes out my nose!

Dad helps us
to calm down.

We breathe slowly.
We count to ten.
The giggles go away.

After lunch,
we see a polar bear.
He is sleeping.

I put my hands
in the air like claws.
I feel big and strong
like a bear.

I pound on the glass
with my pretend paws.
The tour guide points
to a sign.

She tells me
loud noises can scare
some animals.

I stop to think.
Our guide is right.

It is scary to wake up
to loud noises.
I will be more careful.

The last stop of the day
is to see the penguins.
They are my favorite!

I waddle around
with our tour guide.
I thank her for
such a great day.

We pass a park
on the way out.
We stop to play.

I make lots
of funny faces.
My family does, too!

I feel like I am full
of tiny bubbles
about to burst!

My giggles are back.
But now I know
how to calm down
if I need to.

I close my eyes.
It is so much fun
to laugh, play, and
pretend.

What am I feeling?
I am feeling SILLY.

What makes **YOU** feel silly?